Zora Neale Hurston

Philip S. Bryant

Raintree

Chicago, Illinois

© 2003 Raintree
Published by Raintree, a division of Reed Elsevier, Inc.
Chicago, Illinois
Customer Service 888-363-4266
Visit our website at www.raintreelibrary.com

For information, address the publisher
Raintree, 100 N. LaSalle, Suite 1200, Chicago, IL 60602

Printed and bound in the United States at Lake Book Manufacturing, Inc.
07 06 05 04 03
10 9 8 7 6 5 4 3 2 1

Library of Congress Cataloging-in-Publication Data

Bryant, Philip S.
 Zora Neale Hurston / Philip Bryant.
    p. cm. -- (African American biographies)
Summary: Discusses the life and career of the twentieth-century
African-American writer, Zora Neale Hurston.
Includes bibliographical references and index.
 ISBN 0-7398-6872-1 (HC), 1-4109-0041-X (Pbk.)
 1. Hurston, Zora Neale--Juvenile literature. 2. Novelists,
American--20th century--Biography--Juvenile literature. 3.
Folklorists--United States--Biography--Juvenile literature. 4. African
American novelists--Biography--Juvenile literature. 5. African American
women--Biography--Juvenile literature. [1. Hurston, Zora Neale. 2.
Authors, American. 3. African Americans--Biography. 4.
Women--Biography.] I. Title. II. Series: African American biographies
(Chicago, Ill.)
 PS3515.U789 Z635 2003
 813'.52--dc21

                                2002153827

Acknowledgments
The publishers would like to thank the following for permission to reproduce photographs.
pp. 4, 6, 12, 14, 16, 38, 40, 42, 46 CORBIS; pp. 10, 24, 30, 32, 35, 51, 53, 56 Library of Congress; pp. 18, 20, 22, 26, 37, 44, 55 Bettmann/CORBIS; p. 28 Ted Williams/CORBIS; p. 48 © Bradley Smith/CORBIS; p. 58 © Steve Jennings/CORBIS.

Cover photograph: CORBIS

Content Consultant
Dr. Paul Reuben
Department of English
CSU Stanislaus

Some words are shown in bold, **like this.** You can find out what they mean by looking in the Glossary.

Contents

Zora Neale Hurston, pictured here in Florida in the 1950s, wrote several novels and many stories about the African-American experience in the United States.

Introduction

Zora Neale Hurston was one of the great African-American writers of the twentieth century. Most of her short stories, novels, essays, and plays celebrated the rich experience and culture of African-American people.

Hurston was not only a writer, she was also an important **anthropologist.** As an anthropologist she studied the behavior and cultural development of human beings. She was one of the first scientists to collect and study African-American **folklore.** Folklore is made up of the stories and myths that a group of people tell each other. She wrote nonfiction books and articles to explain the things she learned to others.

Much of Hurston's writing was shaped by her experiences during her childhood, which was spent in Eatonville, Florida. This town was one of about 100 all-black towns founded in the United States between 1865 and 1900.

Zora (left, with her back to us) sits on a porch listening to the music of two African-American musicians in Eatonville, Florida, in June of 1935.

Zora is a hard person to fully understand. But if you want to know something about her life and work, all you would have to do is go back to Eatonville. Many of the characters and landscapes in her books were based on real people and places she knew in her hometown. No matter where she went, she always felt that her roots were in the South.

Hurston received many important awards and honors for her writing and studies of African-American folklore. Even so, she was often poor and struggled hard just to pay her bills. It was not until many years after her death that she was fully recognized for the key role she played in the shaping of modern American literature.

Hurston's writing was influenced by the culture of Eatonville and southern Florida. She never stopped writing about these places.

Chapter 1: Eatonville Youth

Zora Neale Hurston was born in Notasulga, Alabama, on January 7, 1891. She was the fifth of eight children born to Lucy Potts Hurston, a former schoolteacher, and John Hurston, a carpenter, farmer, and Baptist preacher.

When Zora was between one and three years old, her family moved to the town of Eatonville. Eatonville was one of the few all-black towns in the South, and it was a refuge from the racial **discrimination** its residents might have faced elsewhere. It was located right in the middle of Florida, five miles from Orlando. About 125 people lived there at the time. The town's mayor, sheriff, and council members were all African Americans elected by the African-American residents.

Eatonville was founded in 1887, 22 years after the Civil War ended. It was the first fully incorporated African-American town.

Zora grew up in the South. She interviewed children like these during a folklore research trip to Georgia.

This means the town had filed the legal papers needed to become an official town, recognized by the state government.

Zora grew up in an eight-room house on five acres (two hectares) of land. Their five acres were full of orange, tangerine, and grapefruit trees. As a girl Zora would play outside, swimming in the nearby lakes and chasing alligators.

Zora was a tomboy. She did not like playing with dolls and other toys that girls her age usually played with back then. She was smart and curious, a bit like Janie, a character she wrote about in *Their Eyes Were Watching God* years later:

> *It was a spring afternoon in West Florida. Janie had spent most of the day under a blossoming pear tree in the backyard. She had been spending every minute that she could steal from her chores under that tree for the last three days. That was to say, ever since the first tiny bloom had opened. It had called her to come and gaze on a mystery. . . . It stirred her tremendously. How? Why?*

Just as her character Janie wondered why the flower bloomed, young Zora was also always wondering about how and why things happened. Her mother, a former schoolteacher, had the strongest influence on her early life. Her mother did not try to change Zora into a prim and proper little girl. Instead, Zora's mother encouraged her daughter's curiosity and answered her questions. Zora was a quick learner. She knew how to read even before she was old enough to attend school.

Zora's mother believed that all her children should receive the best education available to them. They all attended school. At night, Zora's mother gathered them together and reviewed their lessons. She taught them about grammar and how to solve long-division problems.

This is a classroom in Alabama, where Zora was born, about 1902.

When Zora was in the fifth grade, two women from the North visited her school. They were so impressed by Zora's abilities as a student that they sent her a box of books to read. So in addition to her schoolbooks and the family Bible, Zora also had copies of Grimm's fairy tales, Greek and Roman myths, Norse legends, and books by authors Rudyard Kipling and Robert Louis Stevenson. Since Eatonville had no library and African Americans were not allowed to use the libraries in nearby towns, books like these were very precious.

Until late at night, Zora would sit and listen to stories that people told on their front porches. She not only remembered the stories, but also the way people's voices sounded when they told them. She remembered their laughter, songs, and hymns. She did not know then how important those stories would be to her writing when she grew older.

In 1904, Zora's mother died after a serious illness. It was a terrible loss. Her mother's dying wish was that no one should cover up the clock or take the pillow from under her head. These were things that most people in Eatonville did when their loved ones died. They believed that a person would have an easier death without a pillow on the bed, and that if a dying person looked at an uncovered clock, the clock would stop forever. But Zora's mother felt these were superstitions and did not believe them. Zora tried to honor her mother's request, but she was overruled by her father. Zora felt she had let her mother down by not doing as she had asked. Zora saw her mother's death as the end of a happy and important part of her life.

Like the maid pictured here in the early 20th century, Zora had to work for wealthy white people in order to make a living.

Chapter 2:
Leaving Home

Life became hard for Zora after her mother's death. Her father soon remarried. Zora and her stepmother did not get along and often quarreled. As a result, her relationship with her father suffered, too. He often sent Zora to stay with different family members.

During these years Zora did not attend school as regularly as she had when her mother was alive. She had a number of jobs as a maid working for white people in a nearby town. These jobs were often difficult. She did not like serving white people, and she found it hard to act in the humble way they expected. She was a free spirit and longed to return to her books.

No one knows how long this period of Zora's life lasted or exactly how old she was when it began. During her life, Zora gave several different dates for important events in her life—even for the

These African-American women are in a sewing class at Howard University in the early 1900s—about the time when Zora attended Howard.

year of her birth. What we know is that she had to struggle to make ends meet. Zora later wrote about this time in her **autobiography,** *Dust Tracks on a Road*: "There is something about poverty that smells like death. Dead dreams dropping off the heart like leaves in a dry season and rotting around the feet."

When Zora was probably in her twenties, she became a wardrobe girl, taking care of costumes for an actress in a traveling theater company that was touring the South. She stayed with the company for almost two years. While working and touring with the company, she learned a great deal about the world. Even so, she still had a strong desire to return to school and finish her education. She finally left the company while they were in Baltimore. She decided to stay there to finish school.

In September 1917, Zora was accepted at Morgan Academy, a high school in Baltimore. She was 26. She graduated in June 1918 and went on to Howard University. During this period, she worked as a manicurist and a waitress to support herself. She also worked as a maid for distinguished black families living in Washington, D.C.

At Howard University, Zora was admitted into the literary club, the Stylus. In 1921, she published her first story, "John Redding Goes to Sea," in the magazine published by the club. This was the start of her career as a writer. Later, she wrote and submitted her story, "Spunk," and a play about folklife in Florida called *Color*

Fannie Hurst (pictured) was a famous writer who helped support Zora in New York by hiring her as a driver and companion.

Struck, to the 1925 *Opportunity* magazine literary contest. She won prizes in both the drama and fiction categories. Suddenly Zora was a rising literary star and part of a growing community of African-American writers and poets.

Zora left Howard with an associate's degree and moved to New York, taking a job as the personal secretary of Fannie Hurst. At the time, Hurst was a best-selling novelist. Zora turned out to be a very bad secretary, but she was a good friend to Hurst. Hurst hired her instead as a driver and companion because she knew Zora needed a job to support herself.

Hurst introduced Zora to another writer, Annie Nathan Meyer. Meyer was one of the founders of Barnard College, the women's college of Columbia University. Meyer was impressed by Zora and she arranged for her to receive a full scholarship to Barnard College in 1925. Zora was 34 years old.

In her **autobiography,** Zora later wrote that she wanted to do more than "be a grind" (someone who studies a lot) at Barnard. She also wanted to experience the vibrant culture and artistic life in Harlem. She wrote,

I had the same feeling at Barnard that I did at Howard, only more so. I felt that I was highly privileged and determined to make the most of it. I did not resolve to be a grind, however, to show the

Noted anthropologist and professor Franz Boas (pictured in 1931) taught Zora to be an anthropologist.

Franz Boas

Franz Boas is considered by many people to be the founder of modern American **anthropology.** At a time when many **anthropologists** thought of nonwhite people as primitive, he argued that no race was superior to any other. All races, he believed, were equally capable of developing complex cultures.

Boas was born in Germany in 1858 and studied physics and geography before becoming an anthropologist. As a professor at Columbia University in New York City, he taught not only Zora Neale Hurston but also many of the people who went on to develop the field of anthropology in the United States, including Ruth Benedict and Maraget Meade. He encouraged Zora to study her own African-American culture and to record African-American **folklore.** He also helped her get funding for her first such study.

white folks that I had brains. I took it for granted that they knew that. Else, why was I at Barnard?

Zora did well at Barnard. She met a man named Herbert Sheen and they became engaged to be married. She also became interested in anthropology, the study of human societies. Her teacher

African-American poet Countee Cullen, was, like Hurston, another one of the leading writers of the Harlem Renaissance.

was a famous **anthropologist** named Franz Boas. He encouraged Zora to study African-American **folklore.**

But writing was still important to Zora, and her stories continued to be published and to gain recognition for her. She became part of the new literary and arts movement called the Harlem Renaissance, drawing on many of her stories from her early years in Eatonville.

Harlem Renaissance

From the mid-1920s to about 1930, Harlem, a neighborhood in New York City, was an important center for African-American culture. During that time a great many African-American artists, writers, painters, and musicians lived there. The huge amount of work they produced made this period the most innovative and exciting time in the history of African-American arts. Along with Zora Neale Hurston, other important black writers like Langston Hughes, Countee Cullen, Claude Mckay, and Jean Toomer all emerged from the Harlem Renaissance. They eventually became famous both in the United States and around the world.

Zora Neale Hurston (pictured here about 1935) never lost the curiosity she had as a child. She loved learning and was always reading many books on a variety of topics.

Chapter 3:
Success

The Harlem Renaissance was a time when people everywhere, including whites, were interested in Harlem and the African Americans who lived there. This was the world Zora found when she first came to New York City in 1925.

Historians think many white people became interested in knowing more about African Americans during the 1920s for a few reasons. One of these may have been the success of all-black musical and stage shows like *Shuffle Along*, which became a hit on Broadway in 1921. These shows introduced many whites to African-American music, especially **jazz**. They also included dancing, singing, and comedy acts.

The 1920s is often called the "Jazz Age." Many young whites went to Harlem night clubs like the Cotton Club to hear the famous Duke Ellington band. The performers at these clubs were

Duke Ellington (center), known as the "king of jazz," is pictured here with his band in 1931. He was a key musical figure of the Harlem Renaissance.

all African Americans. But these clubs did not allow black people to attend. Blacks and whites could socialize openly together only at private parties, never at public clubs. All-black bands would frequently entertain all-white audiences at clubs located in the middle of black Harlem.

While she was still a student at Barnard, Zora became very much involved in the literary and artistic scene of that period. She was a regular guest at racially mixed parties. There Zora met creative people of all races, including writers, painters, and musicians. Her circle of friends grew larger and now included publishing executives, journalists, and stockbrokers.

At that same time, though, she wanted to continue to be a part of the culture of Harlem. She listened to the street **slang** that Harlem residents spoke to each other every day on street corners and in stores, cabarets, and local barbershops.

She even wrote a glossary of Harlem slang of that time. Here are two of the terms she included:

> *Cut—doing something well*
> *Dig—understand: "Dig me?" means, "Do you get me?"*

In 1926, a literary magazine that mainly published young black writers was organized. It was called *Fire!!* In one issue it published Zora's short story "Sweat." It is one of Zora's finest stories. Other writers whose work appeared in the magazine include Langston Hughes and Wallace Thurman.

Zora and her friends often met to discuss writing and politics. They all wrote about the everyday lives of ordinary African-American people. By doing this, they hoped to bring attention to a group of people that had not yet been written about much in American literature. They wanted to share African-American experiences, sorrows, joys, and hopes with the rest of the world.

This picture of bustling Harlem was taken during the time of the Harlem Renaissance. It was a busy place, full of visitors, traffic, and activity.

Zora had a great sense of humor, but she also had strong ideas about her own writing and that of other African Americans. She believed that all people, no matter what their skin color was, had special gifts to give to the whole world. She did not want her writing to be thought of only as "racial," or to have its only purpose be to improve the position of African Americans in society. She agreed that **segregation** and unfair treatment of black Americans had to stop. However, she did not want art created by black artists and writers to exist only to help her fellow African Americans gain their **civil rights.** Instead, she believed that art should express the deepest feelings and spirit of all human beings, rather than just be put to use for political causes.

As Zora wrote in her **autobiography,** *Dust Tracks on a Road,*

> *Light came to me when I realized that I did not have to consider any racial group as a whole. God made them duck by duck and that was the only way I could see them. I learned that skins were no measure of what was inside people.*

One of the ways that writers deal with difficult things is by writing about them. Years after the fact, Zora wrote about her experience with her mother's death.

from "Mama's Child"

by Zora Neale Hurston

Somebody reached for the clock, while Mrs. Mattie Clark put her hand to the pillow to take it away.

"Don't!" I cried out. "Don't take the pillow from under Mama's head! She said she didn't want it moved!"

I made to stop Mrs. Mattie, but Papa pulled me away. Others were trying to silence me. I could see the huge drop of sweat collected in the hollow at Mama's elbow and it hurt me so. They were covering the clock . . .

"Don't cover up that clock! . . . Lemme put Mama's pillow back where it was!"

But Papa held me tight and the others frowned me down. Mama was still rasping out the last morsel of her life. I think she was trying to say something, and I think she was trying to speak to me. What was she trying to tell me? What wouldn't I give to know! Perhaps she was telling me that it was better for the pillow to be moved so that she could die easy, as they said. Perhaps she was accusing me of weakness and failure in carrying out her last wish. I do not know. I shall never know . . . .

If there is any consciousness after death, I hope that Mama knows that I did my best.

Zora is shown here during one of her first research trips in the South. She felt a strong connection to the people and their stories.

Chapter 4:
Anthropology

Zora's study of **anthropology** led her to believe that black American folk culture held great power and meaning for everyone, not just for African Americans. She had already studied Harlem's **slang.** Now she turned her attention to the folk culture she grew up with in the South. She believed that southern black **folklore** and the people who created it were one brilliant part of the whole of human culture—a part that was equal to anything that came from Europe or anywhere else in the world. She thought that anyone who studied it could learn important things about human culture in general.

Her teacher Franz Boas helped her get a $1,400 award from the anthropology department at Columbia University so she could travel through the South and collect folktales. Because both blacks and women were **discriminated** against, the award was a great achievement for an African-American woman. It showed that other scholars recognized the importance of Zora's work.

Zora began her research when she was in her mid-30s. Toward the end of February 1927, she spent six months doing **fieldwork** in southern Florida. In anthropology, fieldwork means gathering information by observing people and talking to them.

Before Zora began her work collecting **folklore** and folktales, there had been very few studies examining the traditional stories of black southerners. The few studies and collections available at that time were almost always incomplete or put together poorly. In 1927 the field of African-American folklore was wide open. Zora was ready to make her mark.

Zora believed she would be successful because she had firsthand knowledge of the rural black South. Many folklore scholars were white and unfamiliar with southern people and their customs. Because Zora was black and southern, she hoped people would feel comfortable talking to her and sharing their stories.

Things did not turn out the way she expected. When she arrived in Florida, her first attempts to collect stories proved difficult. Zora had picked up a New York accent. She did not sound as if she was from the South, so people were not at ease with her. And people did not know what to make of her questions. Why was she asking them for folktales? Most people lied and said that they could not remember any of the old tales. By the end of March, she had not yet collected many stories. She was beginning to feel frustrated.

These children were photographed while singing a folk song for Zora during one of her field trips to Florida.

She later wrote about her feelings, "My first six months were disappointing. I found out later that it was not because I had no talents for research, but because I did not have the right approach."

Also during this time, Zora married her fiancé of six years, Herbert Sheen. But the marriage was not a success, and they separated shortly afterward. On July 7, 1931, they were divorced.

Part of Zora's funding for her **folklore** research came from the respected African-American historian Carter Woodson. So she was not only doing work for Franz Boas, her teacher, but she was also working for Woodson's Association for the Study of Negro Life and History. She wrote an essay called "Cudjo's Own Story of the Last African Slaver." It tells the story of Cudjo Lewis, a survivor of the African slave trade who still remembered his village in Africa and many of the customs of his people.

At this time, Zora was unhappy with her job as a collector of folklore. She felt her work was forcing her to choose between white or black culture. Zora always believed in the power and wisdom of African-American folk culture. She never saw African-American music, dance, or folktales as less developed than European music, dance, or folktales. But back then, Columbia University was nearly all white. She was moving between two very separate worlds with very different beliefs and standards. Not many university professors

Carter Woodson was an African-American historian who helped Zora do her own research on folklore.

This building in Canal Point, Florida, served the community as a home, store, and juke joint for African-American workers who traveled around working at different labor camps in 1941. This is the kind of place where Zora went to do fieldwork.

thought studying African-American culture was as important as studying European culture. They might have enjoyed **blues** and **jazz,** but they still saw them as less serious forms of music than European music.

It also grew harder and harder for Zora to balance her interest in **anthropology** and her desire to be a writer. She had to decide how to use all the **folklore** she was collecting and she wanted to use it in artistic writing that celebrated its beauty and truth. She began to give up the idea of being a full-time academic. She would be a writer first and an **anthropologist** second.

These farm workers are enjoying themselves by dancing in a juke joint in 1942. Zora often went to juke joints like this while doing fieldwork. She asked people there to share their folktales and songs with her.

Chapter 5:
Collecting Folktales

In spite of her frustration with **anthropology,** at the end of 1927, Zora went on a second field trip to the South to collect folktales. She faced the same problems as she had on the first field trip, but this time she was prepared for them. Instead of approaching people like an educated New Yorker, she reminded herself that she had come from the same place as the people she was trying to study. She had to think of herself as an insider, not an outsider. She started talking in a southern accent again, and tried to speak to the people she met as just another girl from Florida.

For this trip, Zora had her own car and $200 a month given to her by her rich friend in New York, Mrs. Rufus Osgood Mason. Mrs. Mason had an interest in black artists and writers of the Harlem Renaissance. She was a **patron,** which means that she often gave money to artists like Zora.

Mule Bone, *the play Zora and Langston Hughes (pictured) wrote together, was never performed, and their friendship ended. The play was not published in complete form until the 1990s.*

For her research Zora was soon going to **labor camps,** sawmills, and **juke joints** to seek out stories and songs. She made up stories to explain why she wore good clothes and drove a car. This made the people feel comfortable enough to share stories and sing folk songs. She finally became a part of the world she was trying to study. But she had to act tough—and be tough—sometimes. The labor camps and juke joints were rough places where people who worked hard for low pay let off steam by drinking—and often by fighting. Zora often found herself in dangerous situations. She was sometimes present when fights broke out, and at times the fights resulted in the murder of one or more of the workers.

Between 1927 and 1930, Zora collected a remarkable body of African-American folktales, which would eventually appear in her book *Mules and Men*.

In 1930, Zora moved to New Jersey. She continued to edit an analyze the **folklore** she had gathered and she also cowrote a play, *Mule Bone,* with Langston Hughes. The play was a comedy based on a folktale that Zora had collected.

Unfortunately, the two writers disagreed about how the play should be produced and who owned the rights to it. The argument ended their friendship and they never wrote together again. The play was never performed.

This woman is walking out of an employment agency in Florida in 1939. She is looking for a job during the Great Depression.

During the early 1930s, Zora wrote a number of other plays. She even tried acting, playing the part of a cheerleader at a football game. She also worked on a musical show, which was not successful and closed after a short time.

After these setbacks, Zora put together a concert of children's songs, work songs, **blues,** and **spirituals** she had collected. The show was called *The Great Day*. This became her first stage success.

Even though the concert's performances were sold out, Zora did not make enough money from ticket sales to keep the troupe that performed the concert together. The show closed quickly.

When she could not find steady work in New York, she moved back to Eatonville, where she could live more cheaply. The United States was in the middle of the **Great Depression,** and jobs were hard to find. In Eatonville, Zora began collecting folktales and writing fiction again. She wrote short stories, including "The Gilded Six-Bits," a story about how a wife and husband separate, but then get back together again. Published in 1933, it is widely believed to be one of Zora's best short stories. She then began writing her first novel, *Jonah's Gourd Vine*. Zora based the novel on her own family history. The two main characters, John and Lucy, were a lot like her own parents. She was still working on the novel when she ran short of money and took a job as head of the theater

*Zora got a job as a teacher at the Bethune-Cookman college, which was founded by
Mary McLeod Bethune (fifth from right). Bethune is seen here talking to students,
around 1940.*

department at Bethune-Cookman College in Daytona Beach,
Florida. There she organized a performance based on her collection
of folktales. In May 1934, *Jonah's Gourd Vine* was published.

In November 1934, one of Zora's plays was going to be
performed by a theater group in Chicago. So Zora went to Chicago
to help. While she was there, she received money from the
Rosenwald Foundation to continue her studies toward a

doctorate—the most advanced degree a person can earn. However, she decided that going back to school would keep her from her creative writing, which was what mattered most to her. Instead, she decided to travel with another **folklorist** down to Florida to record songs from the region.

Before leaving, she wrote the Rosenwald Foundation to inform them that she was declining the offer of a scholarship. She never did complete her degree at Columbia University.

Zora's collection of folklore, *Mules and Men*, was published in October of 1935. The book was made up mainly of folktales and descriptions of West Indian **voodoo** and hoodoo practices. Voodoo is an African religion that includes many ceremonies and rituals. To hoodoo someone means to perform a ritual to bring that person bad luck. A hoodoo can also be a priest, priestess, or follower of voodoo.

In her collection, Zora presented the folklore in a very straightforward manner. Her own comments on the stories guided the reader, but for the most part the stories appeared just as Zora heard them out in the field. She kept the stories authentic by using the same language people used when they told them to her. Zora thought that this was the best way for others to experience the power of these stories.

To do research for her anthropology work, Zora often attended voodoo ceremonies like this one (about 1950). She then wrote about the voodoo practices in her books.

Chapter 6
Dust Tracks on a Road

In autumn of 1935 Zora worked for a theater project run by
the Works Progress Administration (WPA), a U.S. government
program designed to help artists and writers find work during the
Great Depression. In March 1936, she was awarded a
Guggenheim **Fellowship.** Many artists apply for this fellowship,
which supports them for a set amount of time to work on a special
project, but very few receive it.

Zora used her fellowship to spend time in the West Indies
studying obeah **voodoo,** a form of voodoo linked to West Africa.
She stayed in Jamaica for six months, then traveled to Haiti.
There she learned Creole, the language of the people in Haiti,
and attended voodoo ceremonies and rituals.

She was very moved by the culture and religion of the Haitian
people. She spent hours trying to write down her thoughts after

collecting material in the field. It was during this time that she began to write *Their Eyes Were Watching God*.

Their Eyes Were Watching God turned out to be Hurston's most famous book. It is about a smart, strong-willed girl who was born and raised in a small town in southern Florida. Throughout the character's life, she suffers hardships but stays true to her belief that she should be free to live her life the way she wants to live it.

The book's main character reflects many of Zora's own life experiences and her constant struggles to maintain her artistic freedom. She values being part of a close community but at the same time does not want to give up her independence.

Their Eyes Were Watching God was first published on September 18, 1937. It received very mixed reviews. Most reviewers thought it reinforced negative images of black people. They thought the book used southern black **slang** in order to make fun of black people and the way they spoke. This was not true. Zora's characters spoke the way she heard black people speaking when she was growing up in southern Florida. It would be another 40 years or more before literary critics began to recognize the value of Zora's writing style. Today, many people consider *Their Eyes Were Watching God* to be a truly great novel.

Zora received literary awards for her work, in part because she wrote about real things that she took the time to experience. Here she is taking part in a local musical ritual. Experiences like these gave her material to write about in stories.

After the publication of *Their Eyes Were Watching God*, Zora went to work for the WPA again, this time with the Federal Writers' Program. She received money to work on a book of nonfiction about African Americans in Florida. In June of 1939, she received an **honorary degree** from Morgan State College. Even though Zora had not gone to Morgan State, the college gave her a degree to recognize her achievements. In the summer of 1939, she worked as a drama instructor at North Carolina College for Negroes in Durham, North Carolina. In November, she published a book about Moses. She also continued to make trips into the deep South to collect folktales.

Between April and July, she began writing her **autobiography,** *Dust Tracks on a Road.* It was published in 1942, when she was in her early 50s. She was still outspoken and independent in the book, declaring that she could not be classified by her race alone. She believed she was like any human being, a mix of different traits that made her a unique individual.

Zora received awards for her work. In March 1943, she received Howard University's Distinguished Alumni Award. She continued to publish articles and stories in magazines and newspapers all over the country. She briefly got involved in a Republican congressional candidate's campaign in 1946, for which she returned to New York. Then she traveled to Central America to research black communities and stayed there for almost a year.

Zora declined a scholarship so she could go on this folk-song recording expedition with a fellow folklorist. They went to Georgia, Florida, and the Bahamas. These photos document their experiences and some of the people they met.

Because Zora's writing was not intended to fight for the **civil rights** cause as directly as the work of other black writers and artists, her work was often criticized. She found it hard to earn enough money from sales of her books to pay her bills. In 1950, she had to work for a while as a maid in Miami.

She continued to write throughout the rest of her life, publishing articles in newspaper and magazines. In May of 1956, she received an award for education and human relations at Bethune-Cookman College. She also worked as a substitute teacher at the Lincoln Park Academy in Fort Pierce, Florida.

from "High John the Conquer"   by Zora Neale Hurston

High John the Conquer came to be a man, and a mighty man at that. But he was not a natural man in the beginning. First off, he was a whisper, a will to hope, a wish to find something worthy of laughter and song. Then the whisper put on flesh . . . . The sign of this man was a laugh, and his singing-symbol was a drumbeat . . . . It was sure to be heard when and where he worked the hardest, and the lot most cruel. It helped the slaves endure.

They knew that something better was coming. So they laughed in the face of things and sang, "I'm so glad! Trouble don't last always." And the white people that heard them were struck dumb that they could laugh.

Zora graduated from Howard University (above). The university awarded her a distinguished alumni award in 1943.

Zora plays a drum during a voodoo ceremony. She tried hard to understand the cultures she studied.

In 1959 Zora suffered a serious stroke that left her very ill. She had no money so she had to move to a welfare nursing home. She died there in her sleep on January 28, 1960. She was 69 years old. She was buried in an unmarked grave because she had no money for a headstone.

It was not until a decade after her death that Zora Neale Hurston began to be recognized as one of the great masters of American literature. Her novels, short stories, and folktale collections are now considered classics. They are read and studied by millions of people all around the world.

Zora's stories are mainly set in the deep South, but their messages of human courage, freedom, and love reach far beyond any particular region. Her life and work have become inspirations for writers and scholars of all races and nationalities.

In August 1973, the African-American writer Alice Walker, from the deep South herself, tried to find Zora's unmarked grave. She had long admired Zora's work, and now she wanted to do something to honor her. She planned to place a marker next to the grave, so people could know that a great American writer was buried there.

Walker spent hours searching through tall, snake-infested grass in a field, looking for the grave. When she couldn't find it, she sat down in the grass and started to cry. She was just about to give up,

Alice Walker was inspired by Zora Neale Hurston. Here, Walker gives a speech to encourage African-American people to vote.

she said, when she heard a voice calling her. She got up and walked toward the voice. There, a few hundred yards away, she found Zora's grave, hidden under tall, thick grass. Walker had a marker placed there. It reads, "Zora Neale Hurston, 'A Genius of the South,' 1901–1960, Novelist, **Folklorist, Anthropologist.**"

Written on her gravestone are all of the things that a young Zora Neale Hurston had once dared to dream of becoming. Written on it also is the wrong year of her birth—a fitting tribute to a writer who gave several different years as the date of her birth. During her lifetime, because of her courage and determination, she achieved her dreams.

Alice Walker

Alice Malsenior Walker was born on February 9, 1944, in Eatonton, Georgia. Her parents were poor sharecroppers. She was active in the **civil rights** movement of the early 1960s. She attended Sarah Lawrence College and it was there that she began to write. She has written several volumes of poetry, and her novel *The Color Purple* won the Pulitzer Prize in fiction in 1983. It was made into a very popular movie by the director Steven Spielberg.

Glossary

anthropology   study of the origins, development, and behavior of humans. An **anthropologist** is someone who studies anthropology.

autobiography   biography written by the person it is about

blues   style of music created by African Americans. Blues songs are usually about the struggles of everyday life.

civil rights   personal freedoms that are guaranteed to all U. S. citizens

discrimination   singling something or someone out, often unfairly, because of some feature it or they possess

fellowship   money given to an artist or scholar to support his or her work, also called a scholarship

fieldwork   gathering information by observing and talking to people

folklore   traditional beliefs, practices, and legends of a community, which are handed down by talking. A **folklorist** is a person who researches, records, and studies folklore.

Great Depression   period of time lasting from 1929 through 1939, when millions of Americans lost their jobs

honorary degree   award given by a school to recognize a person's achievement

jazz   style of American music developed by African-American musicians in the early 20th century

juke joints   small gathering places where dances and parties were held in the 1930s

labor camps   camps where people temporarily live and work, often in very bad conditions and for low pay

patron   person who supports an individual or an organization, usually by giving money

slang   unusual phrases and vocabulary often understood only within a small group of people

segregation   separation of African Americans and whites in public places

spiritual   traditional African-American song

voodoo   religion with links to Africa. To hoodoo someone is to perform a ritual to bring that person bad luck.

Timeline

1891: Zora Neale Hurston is born on January 7, 1891, in Alabama.

1904: Hurston's mother dies.

1918: Receives high school diploma from Morgan Academy in Baltimore.

1919–1924: Attends Howard University.

1921: Publishes first short story, "John Redding Goes to Sea," in a campus magazine.

1925: Wins *Opportunity* award with her short story, "Spunk."

1925–1927: Receives scholarship and attends Barnard College, where she studies **anthropology**.

1927: Travels to Florida to collect **folklore**.

1928: Receives her bachelor's degree from Barnard.

1930: Works on *Mule Bone* with Langston Hughes.

1934: Publishes her first novel, *Jonah's Gourd Vine*.

1935: Publishes *Mules and Men*, a collection of African-American folklore.

1937: Publishes *Their Eyes Were Watching God*.

1941: Publishes her **autobiography**, *Dust Tracks on a Road*.

1956: Receives an award for education and human relations at Bethune Cookman College.

1959: Suffers a stroke.

1960: Dies in a county welfare home in Florida.

Further Information

Further reading

Witcover, Paul, C., et al. *Zora Neale Hurston.* Broomall, Penn.: Chelsea House, 1992.

Yannuzzi, Della A. *Zora Neale Hurston: Southern Storyteller.* Springfield, N.J.: Enslow Publishers, 1996.

Yates, Janelle, et al. *Zora Neale Hurston: a Storyteller's Life.* Staten Island, NY: Ward Hill Press, 1991.

Addresses

The Association to Preserve the Eatonville Community, Inc. (P.E.C.)
227 East Kennedy Boulevard
Eatonville, FL 32751

The Hurston/Wright Foundation
6525 Belcrest Road
Suite 531
Hyattsville, MD 20782

Zora Neale Hurston National Museum of Fine Arts
227 East Kennedy Boulevard
Eatonville, FL 32751

Index